W9-ANN-950

Dear Parents:

Congratulations! Your child is taking the first steps on an exciting journey. The destination? Independent reading!

STEP INTO READING® will help your child get there. The program offers five steps to reading success. Each step includes fun stories and colorful art or photographs. In addition to original fiction and books with favorite characters, there are Step into Reading Non-Fiction Readers, Phonics Readers and Boxed Sets, Sticker Readers, and Comic Readers—a complete literacy program with something to interest every child.

Learning to Read, Step by Step!

Ready to Read   **Preschool–Kindergarten**
• big type and easy words • rhyme and rhythm • picture clues
For children who know the alphabet and are eager to begin reading.

Reading with Help   **Preschool–Grade 1**
• basic vocabulary • short sentences • simple stories
For children who recognize familiar words and sound out new words with help.

Reading on Your Own   **Grades 1–3**
• engaging characters • easy-to-follow plots • popular topics
For children who are ready to read on their own.

Reading Paragraphs   **Grades 2–3**
• challenging vocabulary • short paragraphs • exciting stories
For newly independent readers who read simple sentences with confidence.

Ready for Chapters   **Grades 2–4**
• chapters • longer paragraphs • full-color art
For children who want to take the plunge into chapter books but still like colorful pictures.

STEP INTO READING® is designed to give every child a successful reading experience. The grade levels are only guides; children will progress through the steps at their own speed, developing confidence in their reading.

Remember, a lifetime love of reading starts with a single step!

Published in the United States by Random House Children's Books, a division of Penguin Random House LLC, 1745 Broadway, New York, NY 10019, and in Canada by Penguin Random House Canada Limited, Toronto.

Step into Reading, Random House, and the Random House colophon are registered trademarks of Penguin Random House LLC.

Visit us on the Web!
StepIntoReading.com
rhcbooks.com

Educators and librarians, for a variety of teaching tools, visit us at RHTeachersLibrarians.com

ISBN 978-0-593-37390-3 (trade) — ISBN 978-0-593-37391-0 (lib. bdg.)—
ISBN 978-0-593-37392-7 (ebook)

Printed in the United States of America
10 9 8 7 6 5 4 3 2 1

2021 Random House Children's Books Edition

L.O.L. SURPRISE!™

PURR-FECT PETS

by B.B. Arthur

Random House 🏠 New York

So many pets!

Pups! Cats!

Bunnies! Skunks?

No matter what kind you like,

these L.O.L. Surprise! pets

are off the leash!

©MGA

MISS SKUNK

©MGA

Queen Bee's puppy Pup Bee
likes to *bee* fierce.
She looks fetching
in her pom-poms.

©MGA

Ruff Rocker is bad to the bone.

She helps Rocker rock.

Paws up,
Daring Diva!
Daring Doggie
is playing
your song.

Boss Pooch is a boss pup.
Boss Queen takes her
on power walks.

Fancy and Fresh
have *fur*-ever friends.
Fancy Haute Dog is cute.
She loves to be carried.

BFFS

©MGA

Fresh Feline is
Fresh's furry friend.
Who says cats and dogs
don't get along?

XOX

©MGA

Kitty Queen and Kitty Kitty
rock kitty ears.

Not all cats hate water.
Merkitty loves to go to the beach
with Merbaby.

Some pets are pocket-sized.

Splatters loves her skunk

with all her *art*.

Sugar Queen's pets
are small and sweet.
Sugar Squeak
is itsy-bitsy.

Sugar Sneak is
a teeny sweetie.

Punk Boi and Oops Baby

sing with their hamsters.

Punk Hog squeaks
against the machine.

Sometimes Oops Ham squeaks.

Sometimes she rolls.

80s B.B. has 80s babies.

80s Hog just wants to have fun.

80s Bunny is her

best bun *fur*-ever.

Pop Heart has an eye for art.

Hop Heart has an ear for art.

Soul Babe loves hip-hop.

Soul Bun does, too—

especially hop!

©MGA

Some L.O.L. Surprise! pets
have stripes.
Diva, Miss Punk, and Snuggle Bae
love their skunk pets.

Diva Stripes thinks her
stripes hypnotize.
Miss Skunk is a fuzzy
punk princess.
Le Skunk Bébé thinks
waking up stinks.

Some L.O.L. Surprise! pets
have wings.
Unicorn's pony Unipony does.
She believes she can fly.

Bhaddie's monkey does, too.

Bhaddie Monkey knows she can fly.

Fly! Fly! Fly!

Go-Go Gurl's pet

is called Go-Go Birdie.

She flies on flower power.

Yin and Yang keep things Zen
with Yin Hoot and Yang Hop.
Everything is *owl* good
in their *hoppy* place.

Some L.O.L. Surprise! dolls cannot decide on just one pet.

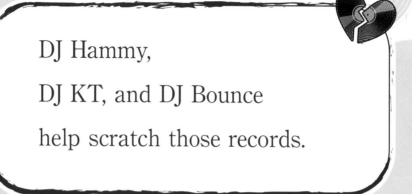

DJ Hammy,

DJ KT, and DJ Bounce

help scratch those records.

ADORBS

Bon Bon has all
the cutest critters.
These pets love
to dress up!
They are all
pretty in pastel.

Neon QT loves every color
and every pet.

Kitty, Hammy, Bunny, Puppy—
she wants them all!

These *paw*-some pets

know how to keep it fierce . . .

. . . and they are *purr*-fect pets!